SOMEDAY

by
Eileen Spinelli

illustrated by
Rosie Winstead

Dial Books for Young Readers

Someday
I am going to be
a great artist.
I will wear a blue smock.
I will carry my paints
to the beach
to paint the sea.
A very rich person
will offer to buy my painting
for two million dollars.
　　But I will smile.
　　　　And I will say: "I'm sorry,
　　　　　　this painting is not for sale.
　　　　　　　It is a gift for my art teacher."
　　　　Someday . . .

Today
I am off to
help my dad
paint the shed.
Green.
(It's where I keep my bike.
I just might paint that too!)

Someday
I will make friends with a dolphin.
I will call her Wilma.
Wilma will let me climb on her back.
We will speed across the water.
We will sail beside tall ships.
We will dip under the waves.
I will ask Wilma
to tell me all the secrets
of the sea.
And she will.

Someday . . .

Right now
I am shaking fish-food flakes into the bowl
where my pet goldfish, Pumpkin, lives.
Pumpkin darts in and out of
his pink castle.
He blows tiny bubbles.
But he doesn't
talk to me.

Maybe goldfish don't have secrets to tell.

Someday
I will dig for dinosaur bones.
Deep in a field
where once a farmer grew corn
and chickens scratched.
I will find the bones of a T. rex.
The farmer will faint
with surprise.
Reporters from the TV station
will bring their cameras
and microphones.
I will be on the evening news.
Someday . . .

Today

I am digging for coins
under the sofa cushions.
Quarters! Dimes! Nickels!
Enough for a Popsicle.

Someday
I will be invited
to the White House
to have lunch
with the president.
He will want my ideas
on world peace.
I will wear white gloves
and a hat with a rose
pinned to it.
I will bring the president
a box of golf balls.
The White House waiter
will pour tea.
I will eat my salad carefully.
No spills on the rug.

In the meantime
I'm having lunch with
my cousin Harry.
Harry talks with his mouth full.
He slurps his milk.
He burps.
I don't think Harry
will ever be invited
to the White House.

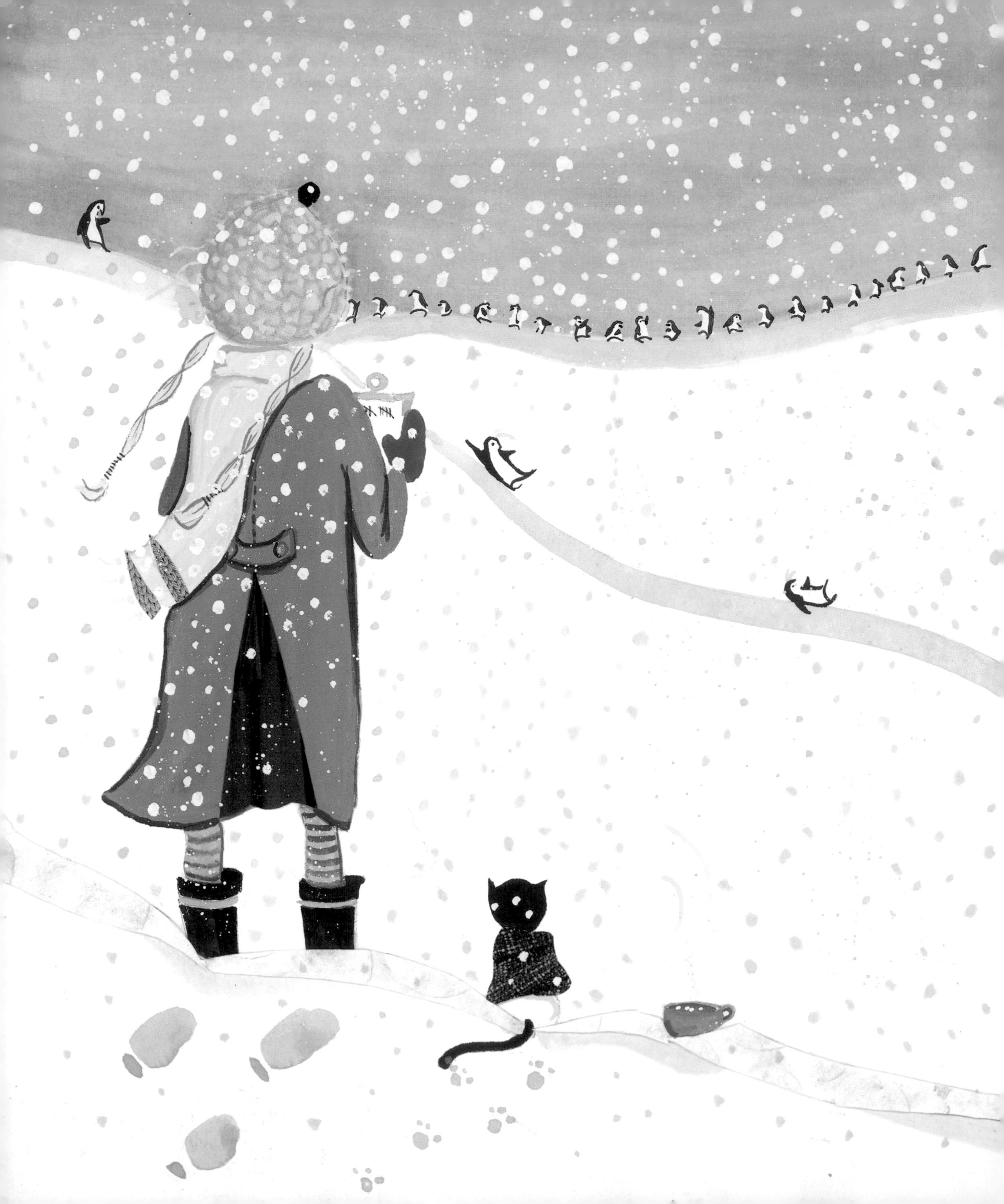

Someday
I will be an animal scientist.
I will travel to the South Pole.
I will count Macaroni Penguins—
all five million of them.
It will take a very, very long time.
My hair will turn gray.
I will return home
to a ticker-tape parade.
Five million people will cheer.

Someday . . .

TO MUM
FROM
ROGER

age 5

Right now
my hair is still brown
and it's jelly beans
I'm counting.
Ten for my
little brother, Roger.
Eleven for me.

One extra for the counter.

Someday
I am going to be
a gymnast
at the Olympics.
I will tumble and
twirl across the mat.
I will leap into the air
as gracefully
as any ballerina.
The judges will swoon
with delight.
I'll win the gold medal!
Someday . . .

As for today—I am practicing cartwheels in the backyard.

Look out!
Splat!

Do they make medals out of mud?

Someday
I will spend the night
in Egypt.
I will ride a camel
in the silvery dark.
I will feel
the cool desert breeze
as I climb down from
the camel's back.
I will take my frog-print pajamas
from my overnight bag
and put them on
behind a thornbush.
I will lie next to the pyramid
in the bright moonlight.
I will dream of golden palaces
and pointy-eared cats.
Someday . . .

Tonight
I'm sleeping
on the bottom bunk
with Roger, who is afraid
of monsters
and the dark.
I think he forgot to brush his teeth.
His breath smells like a camel's.
I turn toward the open window,
where the night sky glitters
with stars.
Quietly Mom and Dad come into
our room to tuck us in.
Mom kisses our foreheads.

When they leave
I go to my window.
I see two baby owls
perched on a branch
of the tree.
I think they are going to fly
for the first time.
In the dark
I smile.
Right now.

To my
little Goldie
— R.W.

To Marianne
Prokop, Millie
Virsak, and
The Twinings
— E.S.

DIAL BOOKS FOR YOUNG READERS • A division of Penguin Young Readers Group • Published by The Penguin Group • Penguin Group (USA) Inc., 375 Hudson Street, New York, NY 10014, U.S.A. • Penguin Group (Canada), 90 Eglinton Avenue East, Suite 700, Toronto, Ontario, Canada M4P 2Y3 (a division of Pearson Penguin Canada Inc.) • Penguin Books Ltd, 80 Strand, London WC2R 0RL, England. • Penguin Ireland, 25 St. Stephen's Green, Dublin 2, Ireland (a division of Penguin Books Ltd.) • Penguin Books India Pvt Ltd, 11 Community Centre, Panchsheel Park, New Delhi - 110 017, India. • Penguin Group (NZ), Cnr Airborne and Rosedale Roads, Albany, Auckland, New Zealand (a division of Pearson New Zealand Ltd). • Penguin Books (South Africa) (Pty) Ltd, 24 Sturdee Avenue, Rosebank, Johannesburg 2196, South Africa. • Penguin Books Ltd, Registered Offices: 80 Strand, London WC2R 0RL, England.

Text copyright © 2007 by Eileen Spinelli
Illustrations copyright © 2007 by Rosie Winstead
All rights reserved

The publisher does not have any control over and does not assume any responsibility for author or third-party websites or their content.
Designed by Teresa Kietlinski Dikun
Text set in Bookman
Manufactured in China on acid-free paper

1 2 3 4 5 6 7 8 9 10

Library of Congress Cataloging-in-Publication Data
Spinelli, Eileen. • Someday / by Eileen Spinelli ; illustrated by Rosie Winstead.
    p. cm. • Summary: A young girl contrasts the exciting things she might someday do, like digging for dinosaur bones and swimming with dolphins, with her present-day activities of finding loose change in the sofa cushions and feeding her goldfish. • ISBN 978-0-8037-2941-4 •
[1. Imagination—Fiction. 2. Family life—Fiction.] I. Winstead, Rosie, ill. II. Title. • PZ7.S7566Sr 2007   [E]—dc22   2004010824